A Battleaxe and a Metal Arm 17:

Hollow Solace

Samuel Fleming

Cover Art by David Leahey

ISBN-13: 978-1-954679-50-4 (paperback)
ISBN-13: 978-1-954679-49-8 (ebook)

Thank you to my Beta Readers

And, as always, to my First Reader,

Mel.

iv

Contents

"This world is an endless black parade. A hollow world of equally empty promises."

—*forgotten*

Previously...

Helesys, Taunauk, and Shawn found themselves in the slumbering bog—the first realm along the path to the Wolf King's throne. The revelations of the prior realms hung heavy on the heroes, but they walked with unbent purpose.

Helesys's revelation of her own death and resurrection was freshest of all. The absent voice of her wand, a painful reminder.

Still, they walked.

The heroes skulked deeper the misty swamp, seeking the seam to the next world. They walked long without interruption, their feet kept above the muck of the bog by Helesys's water walk spell. They fought off the grasping roots of the realm, and saw faces twisted beneath the bark. Before long, they came to a large green cat. It lay in the branches and spoke the common tongue, telling them of the King's path and the witch hunters that lay ahead.

Next, they came to half-buried ruins. There they found their first signs of Terran life, twisted as they were. The witch hunters set upon them without sense or mercy. The heroes held their own until a guardian—a sane hunter—called off the assault.

Beliah was the guardian's name. She led the heroes to an alcove in the ruins. They talked at length, and she told them how the ruins used to be an outpost in the wilds. That Chosen would pass through on their journey to face the Wolf King, but it had been some time since another had come. Other Chosen that stay in the slumbering bog were reduced to madness—like the witch hunters that attacked the heroes. Beliah bid them to follow the ruins, past the Cuckoo's hollow, and to the seam beyond. Beliah would not leave the ruins.

Some time later, the ruins sank beneath the muck. The trees grew larger, their bark twisting and forming caverns through which the heroes passed—the barrows. They walked the winding passages, on guard against the shadows. Soon, they came upon the remnants of a thousand Chosen, twisted beyond repair or sense—the rat-men. Even as the heroes ambushed the first group of enemies, the creatures felt Helesys's magic, like a hive mind.

They ran. Rat-men poured through the cavern after them like an approaching wave. It was everything the heroes could do to evade the tide. As their situation grew dire, they were ambushed by witch hunters. Helesys walled the tunnel with ice, halting the rat-men. She kept the largest waves of creatures at bay with magic. They struggled through the tunnels, beset on all sides by rat-men and witch hunters—it seemed as if the realm itself was against them.

In the end, Helesys used her holding spell against the horde of rat-men, then commanded them as she did the giant manta ray on the hills around the Godpeak. She turned the horde on the witch hunters, and then on itself. She bid them do so until all were dead, save the heroes.

Helesys passed out from exertion and awoke further in the tunnels with her comrades. In the aftermath, they shared their visions and revelations of the prior realms: Shawn of his time as a wisp and as a mortal in the factory. Helesys of her death and resurrection as a made-thing—of the struggle to be whole again. That the three of them all were all looking for Sala Gahenna—the Dungeon. The heroes all sought the elves, for they knew the location of the cursed place.

Their path took them through the Cuckoo's hollow. Helesys felt it like the other lingering deaths, like a festering wound in the realm. A realm of pebbles, oil, and slaves—all illusion. The pebbles were eggs, the oil was ash. Terrans taken over by the Cuckoo.

The Cuckoo tried to assault their minds, but each of the three were immune to its power. After, they easily dispatched the lone mind-controlled Terran, then were surrounded by more. The Cuckoo spoke, but would not yield. The heroes continued on, leaving a pile of lingering dead in their wake.

Deeper into the hollow they went, and the oppressing weight of the space fell on them. They came to a mound—a mountain of shells. More Terran slaves came, and Helesys used her holding spell on them.

The mindspace of the spell was a plane of glass and purple mist—one controlled by the Wolf King. He stepped forward, claiming the Cuckoo as under his protection and granting them passage to the next realm. And daring Helesys to come to his throne room. Helesys returned to the realm, then the heroes walked toward the seam in peace.

In the center of the realm, they found a lone, ancient tree burning in cold blue fire. It spoke with the heroes. Told them that it had been cursed by another Chosen long ago. After some deliberation, Helesys resolved to lift the curse—by taking the cold flames into herself and bonding them to her Ring of Winter. The ordeal strained her painfully, but she succeeded, and turned the curse's power into a boon. In return, the ancient tree healed the scars on Taunauk's ironwood shield, making it nigh indestructible.

With the ancient tree's blessing, they stepped through the seam to the next realm along the King's path.

~ ~ ~

Confluence

Helesys, Taunauk, and Shawn stepped through the seam in the heart of the slumbering bog, and out into the next realm. For a moment, Helesys feared her eyes deceived her—marshland filled her vision.

But this was not the dark hollows of the bog.

The new realm stretched out to the horizon. Streams shimmered in the twilight, and bright green moss covered the land. Above, the sky was the reddish purple of sunset, or perhaps, sunrise. Gentle wind swept past them, carrying a musty smell.

The three heroes stood dumbstruck at the sight.

Shawn said, "This… isn't so bad."

Taunauk sighed—Shawn always gave *breath to fate*. Then Taunauk's mouth fell open. "Do you feel that? The same as on the Godpeak?"

Helesys's magical sense was still extended from walking through the seam. However, she did feel what caught Taunauk's attention. Souls flowed along these streams, their voices growing until they coalesced into a river. It felt to Helesys like she were watching embers swell in a fire. And somewhere far away was the powerful glow of Endroggen souls—

"So many," Helesys said. The souls blazed like a beacon in the night.

Shawn asked, "The missing souls of Accaelum?"

Taunauk nodded, his face quivered. "They *must* be."

"Finally, some good news," Shawn replied. "Let's not keep them waiting."

~

The marshland was not barren as it first appeared. Remnants dotted the landscape: Outlines of buildings, barren tree trunks, decrepit monuments—all worn down and worn bare. The heroes could read nothing left on their faces. Some were so near dissolving that they flickered in the corner of Helesys's vision. In the distance, half-formed mountains crumbled and forests vanished. Taunauk wondered aloud, "What is this place?"

Shawn said, "It reminds me of the plane of dreams. Barely held together illusions. This is what things look like on the borders of dreams or as a dreamer wakes." The rogue's voice grew quiet as he spoke. Apprehensive.

Helesys asked, "You flee when this happens, don't you?" She nodded.

They walked across the marsh realm, held up by Helesys's *water walk* spell. Such a simple incantation, and yet it had seen so much use in the last realms.

They passed through shattered ruins in silence, not wanting to risk ambush in the tight confines, but as they passed to open spaces, they relaxed and talked.

Shawn asked, "What are you both going to do when we finally escape this place?" He juggled his blue bladed dagger as they walked.

There wasn't much for Helesys to think about. When no one answered, she filled the space. "I'm going back to Novissimé to confront my sister, to embrace my mother. Then, I'm going to rejoin the Eternal War, and put an end to it."

Taunauk replied, "I'm going to let go of my charge. Return the souls of my people to Accaelum. Then… live the life that was denied to me."

Shawn glanced sidelong at Taunauk, dagger pausing. "Settle down, start a family, that sort of thing?"

Taunauk smiled—one of hope and not melancholy. "Yes. I think I would like that. And to see my mother, and my shield brother, Thuldreth."

Helesys asked, "What about you, Shawn? What will you do?"

Shawn shrugged. "I think I might try being a god again. *Soldei Milent…* Yeah." He said the name as if trying it on for the first time.

"What about the grandfather and granddaughter from the factory?"

Shawn paused again. "I don't think they're there anymore."

"I'm sorry," Helesys said.

"It's… It's what mortals do. They live short lives."

Taunauk said, "You could come with us."

Shawn scoffed, but the humor slackened from his face as he looked at Taunauk. "Oh, you're serious? I… I don't think I'm cut out to be an Endroggen, and I'd rather not live in a crystalline city for the rest of my days." He smiled. "Thank you for the offer, though. Really."

~

As the fading monuments gave way, streams appeared in their stead, carving across the landscape—growing steadily deeper and more numerous toward the horizon. The trickle of water growing to a roar.

As they neared the first stream, Shawn stooped down. "Do you see this?" he asked, pointing to the surface.

Helesys knelt beside him. The surface of the stream appeared unmoving—not frozen. When water freezes, its surface turned smooth. This stream looked as if it had been cast in glass. It had all the ripples one would expect from water, but *it was not moving*. Stranger still, the stream sounded as if it were flowing.

Shawn pulled a coin from his pocket and tossed it into the stream. As it passed through the surface, the strange illusion was broken and the water resumed flowing as expected. This lasted only a moment before the coin vanished and the water turned eerily glass-like again. All the while, the sound of trickling water did not stop.

"Don't worry," Shawn said. "That wasn't my lucky coin."

Taunauk had been watching over their shoulders. "Is it wise to toss coins into a river of souls?"

"Oh, that's what that is?"

Taunauk nodded, then added, "We should avoid crossing the streams."

Shawn chuckled. "It's not as dangerous as you think. Touching it won't kill us, I mean. But don't go swimming in the deeper rivers to come."

Taunauk's brow furrowed. "Explain."

"This isn't *just* a river of souls… I've seen things like this before."

Helesys asked, "In the dream realm?"

Shawn nodded. "My memories of the dream realm have been more elusive than those of my mortal life, but I think I understand now… Think of dreams as an illusion. The dreamer creates the *illusion* of reality. You look up at the sky, and your mind creates the blue and the clouds and the sunset. Our minds are good at painting in broad strokes—at filling a canvas with illusion. But these," Shawn said as he gestured to the stream, "these are the tiny details that get missed."

Taunauk ran a hand over his short hair. "I understand the metaphor, but why does the illusion break down here? We've seen entire realms perfectly made to fool our minds."

Helesys added, "But we've also seen places where the illusion breaks down. The Cuckoo's hollow, for instance."

Shawn nodded and looked to the horizon. "Yes, but this… This is breakdown on a grand scale. I would not be surprised if the rivers ahead grow even stranger—if the realms to come are even more so."

Helesys asked, "Why?"

"Open your senses again. This time follow the streams."

Helesys did so, extending her magical sense to the streams and the rivers beyond. They wove through the realm like threads of a tapestry—coming from other realms.

Helesys began, "The dead do not die in the dungeon, but once long enough passes, their souls are ground down to nothing, or a little more so. The remnants flow to this realm…" She extended her sight farther down the rivers, feeling them coalesce into steadily larger waterways, until the rivers were roaring with souls. And despite the churning, boiling sound coming from the torrent, the waters were glass-like.

"Not the rivers, "Shawn said. "Further."

She looked past the rivers of souls, to the ends of the realm…

She could see shadows of the realms beyond—blackened planes of ever-lasting darkness and nightmares. Helesys gasped. For a moment, it felt as if she was looking at the dark heart of *Sala Gehenna*—the heart of *the dungeon*. All other realms circled these dark few. All other realms were born from them and returned to them.

Helesys said, "We're heading to the center of the Dungeon." Taunauk eyed them wearily.

Shawn nodded. "The illusions are breaking down the closer we get to the center of the Dungeon. We are in the Dungeon's dark dream, probing into cracks that it has forgotten to paint over. No mortals were meant to walk here.

"We best steal ourselves," the rogue added. "Where we're going, we will see the heart of this wretched place. The last of all the horrible things it has to offer, and the very first stirrings of its evil."

Taunauk said, "Then I am certain that this is where the souls of my people are." When Shawn looked to him, Taunauk added, "They would know which was to go for a good fight."

~

As the heroes walked, the sky and the water grew steadily darker—hued with purple and flashes of lightning.

Even though the clouds were tinged only with the faintest color, Helesys couldn't help but look wearily at the sky. It reminded her of the prior realm—how she'd seen the visage of the Wolf King in a purple realm of fog and glass. Through her mage's intuition, she knew the purple tinge was the remnants of souls passing through the realm. Staining it like pulp.

Terrans began to appear, flickering in and out of sight like the buildings prior. Images of warriors and mages were prevalent. Their garb looked unfamiliar, and Helesys didn't recognize their dress from the short time they existed.

Creatures were much the same. There were fleeting images of wolves, sharks, things that might be rabbits. Twice, the image of a titanic buzzard flickered across the sky. On the banks of the largest streams, serpents twisted around each other. Then there were other creatures only partially formed or too strange to be defined. Like the illusions in the Cuckoo's hollow, these stranger apparitions appeared frequently in the corner of her vision.

The heroes skirted the larger and most solid of the images, though Shawn admitted he didn't know if that would be safer than any other route.

Shawn muttered, "I spy with my eye something… red."

"What is that?" Taunauk asked.

"You're supposed to guess."

Taunauk's brow wrinkled and he gestured to three different apparitions. "It could be any number of things."

Helesys said plainly, "It's a children's game, Taunauk."

The Endroggen grunted. "Since when were you a child?"

Shawn scoffed. "I… I'm not sure. How about… Oh—I'm eternally young! And I saw children's dreams. I was more a child than either of you." Shawn trailed off as he spoke, regret immediately forming on his face.

Upon birth, Taunauk's childhood had been forfeit. He'd been raised as a champion of his people, and without worldly attachment, so that he could be the vessel of the lost souls of Accaelum. It had been the heaviest of burdens.

Taunauk shrugged at the comment, and said plainly, "You weren't the only one to live through others. And besides, to hear Helesys talk, not even *she* had a true childhood."

"It's true," she said. "I was envious of my sister. I was expected to take over House Byyra one day. Aradi had all of our status and privilege, but none of the burden."

Shawn said, "Your mother's still there, isn't she?" Helesys nodded, and Shawn continued, "Time passes differently here… but what about in the real world? How long do you think we've been gone?"

No one answered. Since being imprisoned, they'd met Terrans that had been reborn countless times, beings that might've been hundreds of years or even thousands. But the timelines of their lives seemed abstract. It was doubtful that time passed the same between *any* of the dungeon's realms…

"It's folly to speculate," Helesys said finally, "and it doesn't matter at all if we don't escape."

The hill the heroes walked ended at a short ridge. They peered over and saw a sparse, dead forest. Bare tree trunks flickered in and out of existence. Thick webs stretched between them—cobwebs writ large.

"Oh, Tamir no," Shawn muttered.

"What's the matter?" Helesys asked. "You don't like spiders?"

"Not particularly. Especially not—*stercus*." Shawn's voice shrank to an exasperated whisper. *"Look over there!"*

Shawn pointed through the webs to a shadowy bulge—the shimmering outline of a giant spider. It moved daintily across the webs, half-in and half-out of reality.

Taunauk whispered, "There are more. I count four. Maybe five."

Shawn groaned. "I've seen these buggers before, back in the depths beneath the wizard's tower. I think that was a small one. It wasn't particularly fast, but it could disappear and reappear quick enough to make up for it—not *disappear*, they can go into another plane or something. They're crafty, too." Shawn peered past his comrades, then looked to the other side, toward the growing river.

"There's no way around," Taunauk added. "The forest extends to the horizon, though it's hard to see. We need to go through." Shawn's face grew pale.

Helesys said, "We're not going to let some giant spiders keep us from defeating the Wolf King."

"I know," Shawn said. "It's just… We've all got those things that we don't like. Spiders are one of mine."

"One?" she asked.

"Yes. You forget, I haven't just seen dreams—I've seen nightmares too. There's plenty to be afraid of."

~

The heroes walked the edge of the nearest stream. The streams were growing wider, coalescing into rivers, the nearest more than ten feet across. Though spider webs claimed both sides of the river, the webs didn't cross overtop of the stream.

The three peered into the still and purple waters, looking for signs of danger. When they decided it was safe, they proceeded toward the spider-infested woods, keeping the river to their right side so they wouldn't be surrounded.

Taunauk led them into the barren woods. No one spoke. The wind was dead, and the smell of bark and winter lingered in the air.

Now that they were close, Helesys saw the trees for what they were. They weren't dead or rotten; it looked as if they were partially made. As if something had begun to sculpt the trees and stopped part way.

Or perhaps, was taking them apart.

High above, there were even isolated branches, unattached and hanging impossibly in the air.

The spiders were even stranger up close. Their legs were spindly and long—easily more than ten feet—and their bodies were twice as big as a Terran. They walked across the webs like marionettes, sometimes disappearing completely from view.

They made it nearly halfway through the forest without incident or provocation.

But the webs grew too thick to pass. Blades sliced through easily, and Taunauk and Shawn slowly and carefully severed lines. It might've worked, but the webs were too thick—too many rolls of the dice.

The nearest spider whirled around with eerie grace, then it raced toward them on lumbering strides. Despite its bulk, it was silent, except for the creaks of the webs and the trees.

Helesys kindled power in her metal arm. There were a dozen spells she could use—all powerful, few subtle. Fewer still would dispatch the lone spider without alerting others to their presence.

"*Restu sonmova, temparanea*," she said. The *holding* spell reached out, and the spider vanished. Helesys couldn't feel its mind. "I can't hold it."

"Yeah," Shawn muttered. He was still slicing through webs with his dagger. "They're tricky like that."

Helesys scanned the treeline, waiting for the spider to reappear. "Anything else I do is going to give us away."

Taunauk was slicing through webs with his axe. "Let us know if they get close."

Helesys leveled her gauntlet. The spider reappeared fifteen feet away, mandibles chittering. She let loose three blasts, but the spider vanished before any struck true. As her blasts careened through the trees, Helesys caught signs of more movement. "More will be upon us soon."

She kindled a spreadblast in her gauntlet—a dense spray of arcane energy that was both powerful and wide. It wouldn't travel far, so Helesys waited for the last possible moment.

The spider reappeared in front of her—fangs nearly close enough to touch her metal hand. Helesys fired. The spider burst like a sack. When the flash of purple faded, green blood and entrails sloshed across the ground and legs tumbled over like felled saplings.

Helesys readied another blast. "That wasn't so tough."

Shawn groaned, "Breath to fate! They're crafty."

Five spiders—*at least* five spiders—lumbered through the trees, blinking in and out of existence. Right toward them.

Helesys altered her spell. "Fine. Let's see how they like fire. *"Immotalem Immortalis!"*

Fire leapt from her gauntlet, fanning out and spreading like a tidal wave across the woods. The barren trees caught flame like oiled torches. Webs melted. She compounded the spell with the Gar of Shéslang, and the inferno grew. Helesys winced at the heat and kindled strength. Beside her, Taunauk turned golden—bolstered with the strength of his ancestors.

Shawn cried out in surprise. "There are more behind us!"

Helesys spun around and saw more spiders approaching from across the stream. They skittered in a frenzy toward them, despite the fire.

This time, she called on her Ring of Winter. What once had been a tendril of frost lurking inside her had grown into veins that threaded throughout the length of her body—a boon of power salvaged from the curse of cold fire. Helesys felt the crystalline ring respond accordingly.

"Murum glaciei tempestatemque!" Helesys commanded. Frost leapt from her elven hand and spread across the stream, but this time there was no pain, no unpleasant grating of her nerves—the tendril of frost stayed within her, bound to her. Ice spread across the bank of the stream, growing upward and forming a wall forty feet high and a hundred feet long.

Helesys smirked. So the suffering under the curse had tempered not just her, but the Ring of Winter, as well.

Through the ice, she could see the faintest outline of spiders as they struggled to climb and failed.

"We must go!" Taunauk shouted.

The webs blocking their path had fallen, severed by flames. To their left, the fires raged, burning through the rest of the trees and webs with terrifying speed.

The heroes ran, webs disintegrating to ash around them.

But the fire burned out quickly, and as the flames died, the giant spiders came for them. Fangs appeared in front of Helesys, spread wide—

Helesys ducked and slid beneath the giant spider. As she skidded across the ground, she swung her spear hard, and two legs of the beast shattered. She rolled out from under the spider and it chittered in pain. Helesys raised her gauntlet and let loose a spreadblast that burst the creature.

Another spider emerged from the flames, skittering toward Taunauk. The barbarian roared and leapt toward the creature, axe swinging overhead in a powerful arc—but it vanished! The spider and barbarian passed through one another harmlessly.

It reemerged as soon as it passed Taunauk, and continued sprinting toward Shawn.

The rogue's eyes went wide, and he tugged at his arm wrappings. The black bandages fell half-free and seemed to hang in the air. Shawn became a blur, stepping between and slashing at the spider's legs. It stumbled and fell, its momentum carrying it directly into the stream. It crashed into the waters and disappeared.

Helesys turned and reeled, narrowly avoiding the mandibles of another beast. She kindled strength and speed in addition, ducking and weaving while readying another blast. Twice she nearly fired, but this spider was quicker—flickering in and out of existence in the blink of an eye.

Shawn had been right. The bastards were clever *and* they could learn.

More spiders set upon them, and her comrades became flashes of steel. Helesys lunged forward with the Gar of Shéslang, and the spider reeled from her, dancing backward like a flailing marionette.

Beyond, she caught glimpses of Taunauk and Shawn as they attacked the same spider from in front and behind. Taunauk managed to catch it unaware, splitting its abdomen in two with his axe.

Spiders came in flashes. Helesys whirled, spinning with her spear and blasting repeatedly. But nothing struck. The spiders grew smarter, more cautious.

On a whim, Helesys's metal arm bent backward behind her and let loose a spreadblast—the remnants of a spider crashed to the ground.

But even that wasn't enough. Soon her spear and her blasts hit nothing but air. Even beyond, Taunauk and Shawn shouted in frustration.

Then the golden glow around Taunauk flared. His eyes blazed so bright they looked like white stars plucked from the sky.

As Helesys recoiled from the spiders' relentless assault, she heard the horrid slash of axe rending arachnid. Moments later, the spiders around her were cut in half.

Taunauk loomed large over them like a golden bonfire. He turned to face the last of the spiders. Afterimages of other Endroggen followed his wake. Taunauk raised his axe and waited—Helesys and Shawn stood still, watching.

Half a dozen more spiders lumbered toward them like flickering ghosts. Taunauk waited.

As the spiders reached him, the Vessel of Accaelum moved in flashes—like gold lightning. Taunauk moved as if he were possessed, pausing in between each mighty slash—not bothering to reset his stance or block a spider that could appear out of nowhere.

Taunauk could see. There was no hiding from his wrath.

One by one the spiders fell. Cleaved in half.

The last spider stopped short. Then turned and fled through the smoldering woods.

~ ~ ~

The Damned Pyramids

Helesys, Taunauk, and Shawn strode through the aftermath of their battle—across the lifeless riverbank.

Shawn turned to Taunauk. "That was some trick. Care to share with the class?"

Taunauk's golden glow had long since faded, but his face was weary. Troubled. He didn't answer, and merely strode a few steps quicker, until he walked ahead of them.

Shawn leaned toward Helesys to ask, "What's wrong? I thought that was a great showing back there…"

"He'll talk when he's ready." Helesys meant it, but she worried for her comrade. His entire life, Taunauk had borne burdens for others. He had stayed silent and stoic. Forged from stone.

Shawn said quietly, "Terrans weren't meant to bear such weight—of a life deferred and ancestors long dead. One life brings enough hardship."

"Coming from a god?"

"No," Shawn replied. "Coming from a man who merely tried to live two lives."

~

The heroes walked on and the river grew wider. The water grew darker until it was a deep purple. The sound of churning water became ever-present, though the water did not move. Always, the river looked like a still-painting.

Above, the sunset was long gone. The sky grew dark and cloudy. Faint carried ozone, as if a storm were hiding on the horizon.

The soft ground was laden with glass, and it crunched beneath their boots. Most was clear, but every so often Helesys spied a rainbow of glass shards and thought it might've been the last remnants of a long-forgotten church—though it was hard to imagine anything ever surviving there. The eerie waters and shards of the past called to mind a god sweeping their hand across the land, like an artist might wipe away a canvas.

Though they walked in silence and with weapons ready, it felt as if they walked through a graveyard. Everything was dead and buried. Harmless—or so it seemed.

In the distance, the river flashed bright purple, like lightning coursed beneath it. Helesys could just make out a black pyramid straddling the river. Other peaks dotted the horizon.

The seam lay beyond.

Vaguely Terran forms appeared in the distance. On their heads rose great sets of antlers, nearly as large as the creatures were.

Helesys opened her magic sense and realized them familiar. She turned around, and found herself staring face to face with one of the creatures. This time she didn't kindle power.

The creature's skin was moss green, and shimmered intermittently with color, as if it too had glass beneath its surface.

Its skin was without shade or line of muscle, and its head towered above them. There was the faintest line of lips and nose, and eyes were spheres of bright green. Above them, its antlers were twisted brambles of vine and branch that hid sacred runes within.

They had met the creatures on the foothills of the Godpeak, but back then they had taken a form of ice and snow.

The creature craned its neck to look down at Helesys. Its voice was rustling leaves and a snap of branches. *"You are not afraid."*

Helesys kindled voice. *"We have seen your kind before. We parted without incident."*

"You are not afraid of this place."

"One can be afraid, and still journey forward," she replied. When the creature didn't reply, Helesys asked, *"Do you remember what you are? Can you tell us anything about his place?"*

"We are watchers. We have seen much and remember so little. I watched my elders bend the Jesire to their will. I saw the last of the Dreadgods fall and cry molten tears, then walked the ashfields in its wake. I watched our twin stars die and sailed the cosmos in the dark and in the cold.

"I have watched, *young one. So when I say there is no solace here, you should believe it.* Nothing *can prepare you for what lies beyond the River of Souls, the pit in the heart of this place. You should be afraid."*

The creature fell backwards like a tree being struck down, and when it hit the ground, it faded into leaves. Moments later, they crumbled and blew away. Its brethren on the horizon were gone.

Taunauk and Shawn looked at her expectantly.

Shawn said, "One of these days, you need to figure out how to include me in the conversation."

Taunauk asked, "What did it say?"

Helesys shook her head. "Nothing helpful."

~

As they walked, Helesys told her comrades what the watcher said—that only horror lay ahead of them in the heart of the dungeon.

But Helesys felt she was beginning to understand it.

While they walked, Helesys said, "Zinric, the elder mage of Civirrea confirmed that the Gatekeeper—now, Queen—was the original ruler of the dungeon. But the Wolf King usurped her. Perhaps this, *all of this*, is his doing." She gestured to the decaying landscape.

Shawn added, "That would explain all the Chosen over the years. She couldn't do it herself, but she kept trying. She kept gifting power to others that wound up trapped here."

"There's more," she said. "Back in the Wode, the Green Knight spoke of the Gatekeeper as if she were merciful, even kind. But that changed when she met the knight that would become the Wolf King. He didn't just usurp her. He corrupted her. Turned this place into a nightmare."

"You think so?" Shawn asked.

Helesys replied, "He's protecting the Cuckoo. Any Terran that harbors a lingering death like that is capable of anything."

Taunauk said, "The Wolf King sits on the throne, but not for long. Perhaps we can do more than escape… Perhaps we can set the realms right."

"Perhaps," Shawn said. A tentative look flitted across the rogue's face. "Taunauk, do you remember what the elder tree asked of me, last realm?"

"Yes," the Endroggen replied solemnly. "What of it?"

Shawn continued, "It asked if one should suffer forever for their misgivings. I think that counts for you, as well. You're hard on yourself for something you had no control over. For no fault of your own…"

"It is not the same," Taunauk said. "My task is not finished."

Helesys added, "Just because you must suffer, doesn't mean you need to suffer alone, or in silence. Confide in us."

"I do not want their help," he said.

"Why not?"

Golden light appeared beside them. The spirit of Taunauk's father, Rehkoros, stood on the bank of the river. He was clad in Endroggen furs. His face was a wrinkled mirror of Taunauk's, his hair and beard both long and braided. Contrasted with Taunauk's face, shorn to stubble and weary—even then, Taunauk overshadowed his father.

Rehkoros said, "You must let the spirits aid you."

"Shouldn't I be doing these things by myself, athair?" Taunauk didn't meet his father's eye.

His father sighed and nodded to Helesys. "Even your friend says as much. You should listen to her. She is wise beyond her years."

"*Please*… leave me alone."

Rehkoros paused as if he'd been struck. Then his face hardened. "No. You are my son, and I am here whether you want me here or not."

Taunauk turned, teeth grit in frustration. But when his eyes met Helesys's, she saw only pain behind them.

"Talk to him." The words came were perhaps sterner than she meant.

Rehkoros asked, "Do you resent us, balac? Do you resent me?"

"No," Taunauk said quietly. He turned. "You did what you thought was necessary. But you did so out of fear. You did all those things and denied me all those things *out of fear.* Our people are not supposed to act out of fear."

"I'm sorry—"

"I am a broken man, athair! I am a shell. I am… *exactly* what I was meant to be," Taunauk bellowed, and it felt as if the ground shook.

Rehkoros stepped forward and grasped his son's shoulders, looking up into his eyes. "And when this is over, you will be something else."

"What?"

"Whatever you choose to be."

Rehkoros embraced his son, golden tears welling up in his eyes. Slowly, Taunauk embraced him and laid his head on his father's shoulder.

Helesys pulled Shawn by the arm, and the two of them walked up the still-river in silence.

~

Helesys and Shawn walked over the next hill and stopped beside the river—a respectful distance away.

Shawn glanced back at Taunauk and his father. "Do you think they'll be okay?"

Helesys turned away and looked out toward the ends of the realm. Toward the seam. Black pyramids dotted the horizon.

The elven weaver shook her head. In truth, she didn't know if Taunauk or his father would be alright.

The moment dragged on, and Shawn said, "A copper piece for your thoughts."

"How many realms do we have left?"

Shawn's brow wrinkled. "A few, maybe."

Helesys said, "How many days does it take to mend a year's wrong? There is so much pain between them. Decades of it. How fast do you think they could repair their bond? Even if they truly wanted to, Rehkoros will leave once we escape. I do not know how easy it is to commune with the dead, but I imagine Taunauk will never have this chance again."

"Not while he lives," Shawn replied. Helesys shot him a look, and Shawn added, "What? It's the truth. When Taunauk passes, he'll go to Accaelum with his father."

"That is a *grim* point."

Shawn shrugged. "My father died making me. I didn't know the old man… Either way, I think Taunauk and his father will be alright, even if they don't have time."

"How can you be so sure?"

"Because they want to mend things. Sometimes *wanting* is enough. The rest will take care of itself."

Helesys smiled. "That's surprisingly wise."

Shawn held up two fingers. "I've lived two lives to your one. Don't feel bad. What about you? Do you want to mend things with your sister, Aradi?"

The weaver's smile faded.

She felt akin to Taunauk, though thankfully Helesys didn't have the specter of her sister bound to her. No, Aradi was as far away as a sister could be. She was in the real world, while Helesys was trapped.

For some reason, Helesys had been searching for Sala Gahenna—the dungeon. Perhaps there were rumors of healing—something to make Helesys whole again. Aradi had found the dungeon for Helesys. Had Aradi really done so out of a sister's love, or did she have another motive?

Every time Helesys imagined her sister, Aradi always wore a viper's sneer.

"I know what the right answer is," Helesys finally said. "But I don't trust her. The more memories return… I don't think I've ever really trusted my sister. What of you? Have you given any thought to whether you'll become a Terran or a god again?"

Shawn shrugged and looked wistfully across the horizon. "Still figuring that out."

~

Taunauk joined them by the river a few moments later, his cheeks still drying, but standing a little straighter. Wordlessly, the heroes continued down the moving and not-moving river.

Helesys smiled faintly. If only one of them should have closure, she hoped it was Taunauk. She had no reason for the thought—all three of them were strange fellows bearing even stranger struggles. And all three of them, at times, seemed liable to collapse under their own weight. But she and Shawn had at least known some respite, even if it was long ago when they were young.

The words came back again: *One should not have to suffer forever.* Her comrade was owed respite.

As the heroes walked, they were flanked on both sides by rivers. Their waters were still frozen, though the sound of flowering water had grown to a roar befitting their size. The two rivers on either side of the heroes met in the distance, beneath one of the black pyramids. The pyramids loomed large, rising up several hundred feet high and even wider. Three of the structures straddled the rivers, their bases overlapping, and their ends reaching out nearly to the ends of the horizon.

It wasn't until they neared the central pyramid, that Helesys realized the rivers were not the only things making noise. A howl came from the pyramids, like a roaring cyclone. Helesys kindled strength as they approached, and the painful howl became merely deafening.

They neared the foot of the central pyramid, the obsidian wall blotting out the red sky. The face of it was cold, slick stone. Helesys peered into it, expecting to see her reflection, and instead saw nothing but seamless black, as if the stones let not even light escape.

Helesys felt a tap on her shoulder, and saw Shawn pointing at a doorway in the wall. The noise was far too loud to talk over, so Helesys tilted her head in question. She was sure the doorway hadn't been there moments before.

Shawn shrugged, then pointed to Taunauk. The Endroggen was staring up the face of the pyramid, looking at some indiscernible spot. Helesys tapped his shoulder, and Taunauk snapped out of his trance. They followed Shawn into the black pyramid.

~

Darkness stretched out before them, sleek black walls disappearing into the gloom. As soon as Helesys stepped beyond the threshold, all sound ceased—no rushing water, no howling wind, no footsteps.

The warm smell of ozone was so strong it made Helesys's eyes water, even with kindled strength.

Helesys held up her metal arm and conjured its *warding light*. A narrow passageway stretched into the distance—impossibly faint. Again, the light seemed to die as it fell upon the sleek obsidian walls.

Taunauk turned and opened his mouth, but no sound came out. Unperturbed, he pointed to his eyes, then down the hall, then to Shawn and behind them, signaling which directions they should watch.

Helesys and Shawn looked behind them, and found the doorway already gone. Only shadow remained, as if the pyramid had swallowed them up.

Shawn frowned, slipped a dagger from his ethereal pouch, and carefully touched the blade where the entrance had been. He tapped it several times against the wall. No sound echoed, but Helesys thought she saw the white blade flash a little brighter in the *warding light*. Shawn shook his head and gave up.

Then Taunauk stalked forward down the hall, shield and axe ready. Helesys followed with Shawn behind her.

Only a few steps later, the walls began to move. At first, the movement was so faint that Helesys thought it's a trick of the eye. But the shadows writhed—churned—like a school of serpentine fish just beneath the black. The movements in the walls were never more pronounced than shadows, but they were there. Even Taunauk glanced at the wall, uncertainty written on his face.

It was only the walls nearest her light that showed movement. Down the hall in either direction, the walls were sleek and endlessly still. Helesys let her eyes linger for a moment as they walked and decided that the movements weren't random; there was order. Pulsing. Turning. Spinning.

Perhaps the warding light was pushing at the fabric of the place. Helesys decided that she was seeing gears and machinery beneath the walls, like silk stretched across forged shadows.

A scream broke the silence, ringing high like whining glass and was gone even before the heroes flinched. It came from down the long hall. Silence settled in the pyramid again.

Finally, the hall opened up. The black hallway gave way to a cylindrical cavern some fifty feet tall and just as wide. The heroes walked on a black platform that seemed to hang in the middle of the room, while the purple river ran beneath them. Whatever magic lingered in the pyramids had changed the river; now it churned and sloshed beneath them, its waves crashing against the edges of the walkways. Shimmering light filled the cavern, muting the shadow clockwork.

Silence still reigned, save for those shrieks of glass. Every few minutes, the horrid sound would tear through the passageway, accompanied by a flash—purple lightning coursing through the waters. Each was accompanied by afterimages of unrecognizable ghosts hanging in the air around them. Helesys squinted against the bright light and saw the walls in earnest: A deep cobweb of otherworldly gears spun behind the obsidian walls.

Even the living ship of the Idnauthi had not felt so strange and alien.

Miles they walked, and the cavern stretched on.

A flash of movement in the distance. A tattered shadow moving closer. It lurched like a cloth caught in the wind. In moments, it moved a hundred feet.

Helesys thought of the marionettes in the abyssal palace beneath the endless sea. But these were made of shadow, save for the ends of their limbs—its arms ended in glistening white sickles. And like the previous marionettes, strings of shadow connected them to the walls like spiders' webs.

Shawn tapped Helesys's shoulder, and she knew that there were more coming from behind them. They came in ghostly silence and with a nightmare's quickness.

Helesys kindled strength and speed, and waited. Taunauk's body glowed a brilliant gold. She had no doubt Shawn did similarly behind her.

A flash of purple lightning coursed through the river, bringing with it a scream, and the sound of the marionettes—shadowed strings snapping like whips. Then the light and sound faded again, and the battle began.

Taunauk and Shawn met the shadows in flashes of steel—for the moment, Helesys kindled her power and watched.

Their powers had grown in the last few realms. Before, Helesys would've bolstered her comrade's powers against such foes. But now, Taunauk and Shawn held their own. Dagger and axe found the slender strings that powered the marionettes and severed them with expert violence. The shadowy creatures slumped over and then collapsed as their tethers disappeared, before vanishing in puffs of shadow.

Their numbers grew, and Helesys readied her fire. "*'Immotalem Immortalis!'*" But no sound escaped her lips, and the spell died on her metal fingers. Helesys seethed and met them with the Gar of Shéslang, slipping their blades and slashing the strings. It was woefully slow compared to her fire.

As her enemy fell, Helesys readied her gauntlet, then sent purple blasts down the cavern. These bursted harmlessly around her targets. She could conjure some powers wordlessly. Why not others?

Helesys focused herself and thought of fire. She didn't need a fireball. Even the thinnest strand of flame would do. Her gauntlet grew warm, like when she churned power. She focused on the strings.

Immolate, she thought. Wisps of flame appeared, like trails of an invisible sword. She repeated the old word in her head and commanded fire, striking down each strand of shadow. At first, the strokes of flame were unwieldy, but as each marionette is cut down her command grew steady—

Until she was one with flames. They came with the speed of thought.

The shadowed marionettes sprung from walls, thick as flood water, and crashed upon a dam of magic and steel.

When the storm of marionettes finally retreated, the heroes walked the rest of the pyramid in tentative peace, occasional streaks of lightning their only measure. The further they walked, the brighter the water and the coarser the screams.

~ ~ ~

River of Souls

The heroes emerged from the obsidian pyramid into a riverbank beneath a starless sky. A cold breeze blew across the river, the contrast stark compared to the warm air just moments ago.

Beside them, the river had grown wide and now stretched out nearly a thousand feet. It was still and crystalline again, and now the whole of it was brilliantly lit like a raging lightning storm.

But now the water was quiet—muffled—as if something had been stripped from it.

"By Tamir," Shawn muttered. The rogue was staring out across the river. Then he knelt beside it, as if he wanted to reach out and touch the surface but his hands were curled in pain. His voice grew hoarse. "The pyramid *changed* them..."

Helesys and Taunauk knelt beside their comrade and waited for him. Taunauk looked at him worriedly—urgently.

"Souls come here from all over the dungeon," Shawn said. "Once they finally tire from death and rebirth, when they have no will left, they come here. They flow through the pyramids and... this place grinds out the last remnants of who they were.

There's nothing left of them now. No joy, no memories, no person… no dreams.

"This is what we saw," Shawn said, voice growing quiet. "This was the light from the end of the realm. What we're seeing is what's left of *everyone*. Raw ether."

Taunauk turned away and looked off into the distance.

Helesys opened her magic sense, reaching out for anything—anyone left—be they Endroggen or other. But she could feel nothing beyond the river. Nothing but thousands of breathless screams. Even the seam felt shrouded by the turmoil that flowed beside them.

She asked, "Taunauk, do you feel—"

"I feel nothing." The Endroggen bowed his head. "Ancestors forgive me. We were too late."

The golden figure of Taunauk's father appeared kneeling beside him. "All is not lost, balac. We will find what is left, be them shattered or broken. Carry them, if we can. If nothing else, their strength will be our strength. We will reforge them and set them to new purpose within you."

Helesys's gaze followed the river to the horizon, where its waters seemed to bleed out to a smoldering purple landscape.

Rehkoros's words gave her hope, but stronger than hope were her questions.

~

The heroes pushed aside their weariness and continued on. The ground became sludge—a mix of crunching glass and muddy earth. Helesys cast *water walk*, and the three hastened across the realm. Even though sound had returned, silence settled between them. Hope was scarce, and so duty and necessity pushed them on.

Helesys scanned the horizon for danger and thought only of the seam. So, she nearly stopped mid-stride when an obelisk appeared in the distance. It was the same deep black as the pyramids, but seemed to reach up to the very height of the night sky and radiated menace.

As they grew closer, the sleek monument looked more like the sky had fractured.

"Someone's there," Taunauk said, stopping suddenly. He pointed with his axe. "By the river."

They approached slowly. Though the area around the obelisk and the river was desolate, they took no chances. Helesys felt nothing amiss with her magic sense, and yet dread filled the air—felt as if it seeped through her armor and clung to her skin.

A Terran knelt by the river, clad in armor. The silver was marred by shiny black in streaks and patches—like diseased vines or moss. Their sword and shield are void-black. As the heroes neared, the figure stood and turned to face them. Beneath the armor, one side of the woman's face was pale, the other gleaming obsidian.

"Long ago a Gatekeeper passed through here," the knight said. Her voice melodic as a song and carried the smell of death on it. "She was raven-haired and fair. Ungodly beautiful and equally kind. She wanted for one thing, for *all things* to share her warmth…"

"*You!*" Taunauk said.

In the wode, many realms ago, they had come upon a green knight who mourned the loss of her Gatekeeper. Helesys and Taunauk faced her, and Taunauk had perished by her blade. But not before Helesys blighted her and severed the knight's druidic-like powers.

The knight continued unperturbed, "She left me… Left us lowly creatures with only fading memories of times inexorably forgot."

Shawn whispered, "You guys know this… lady?"

The knight looked to each of them in turn, her eyes lingering on Taunauk and then locking on Helesys. "Perhaps my queen hasn't forgotten about me. She's delivered me my spoils."

Helesys called, "She's delivered you nothing but ruin. Don't you see where you are? Or have you gone blind?"

She scoffed. "Far from it. I searched for her. A hundred lives and thrice as many realms I've searched. But my queen no longer wanders the halls of her castle… I am closer to her now than I have ever been."

Taunauk squeezed the pommel of his axe. "You've gone mad."

"*Enough*," the knight said, and the wind died. "I know what you are—that you're Chosen to face the King. *Fools*, and three of many. Only those *I deem worthy* will pass." She smiled. "How fitting that the clanless and the false-elf stand before me once again."

"Get out of our way," Helesys said. "Unless you want a repeat of our last battle."

"I should thank you, weaver. Without you, I would've stayed in the wode, instead of seeing the truth." The knight raised her sword. "Let me thank you, properly."

Helesys kindled power in her gauntlet. "So be it—"

"No," Taunauk said. "She is mine."

Helesys and Shawn stepped back hesitantly. Taunauk raised Everfall and his axe.

"Come to die again, outlander?" the knight asked, a coy smile on her face.

"Your faith has blinded you. You walk a false path and cling to empty purpose. One as pious as you cannot afford to be wrong—No. I journey through the realms so that I might live again. So that my ancestors might live again. And you *are in my way.*"

"So be it. *Manes de lapsis.*"

Terrans in black armor rose up around the knight—dozens of them—their faces twisting into mirrors of her own. They ran at Taunauk, and the barbarian smoldered with golden fire. Endroggen spirits sprung from him and clashed with the black knights.

Taunauk strode forward. Twice he raised weapons against the clones, then he stopped. Obsidian blades struck him, and for a moment, Helesys feared for her friend. But as the blows fell upon his shoulders, his neck, his arms, each clone that struck him exploded in a flash of golden light. Taunauk's golden warriors faded—no longer needed.

The knight frowned, then dove into the growing mass of clones. There was no telling them apart from afar—not without magic.

Taunauk's eyes blazed bright, as if his soul raged and poured through his sockets. He peered through the crowd, unperturbed by the clones striking him and exploding. Then he raised Everfall as a void-black sword crashed down—a horrid clang echoed across the riverbank.

"Shadows and tricks!" Taunauk shouted, staring her down. Then Taunauk and the real knight fought, and the rest of the clones dissolved into smoke.

"*Subita morte.*" The knight disappeared—

And reappeared behind Taunauk, ready to plunge her sword into his back.

Helesys's heart dropped. She reached out with power, ready to *hold* the knight—too slow!

A golden figure sprang from Taunauk's back, pushing aside the knight's sword and shoving her backward. Taunauk's father, Rehkoros, stood tall, face twisted with rage.

"Blasted barbarians!" the knight howled.

The knight became flashes of movement, moving in stuttering blinks—appearing before Taunauk one moment and Rehkoros the next. Father and son fought back to back, yielding nothing. Then their eyes glowed with golden light, and no longer did they merely block and parry. They struck at the knight moments before she appeared—anticipating her movements.

A cacophony of blows rained across the riverbank, neither party yielding.

Finally, the knight stopped and leveled her sword at the pair. "No more powers. No more magic or ancestors. You and I, alone, outlander."

Rehkoros looked to his son, but Taunauk held the knight's stare. Reluctantly, the father faded, leaving his son alone and without the help of his people.

Knight and Endroggen rushed forward and met each other with fury.

When the two had fought before, in the depths of the wode, the knight had used a grounding spell to anchor and strengthen her. No matter how strong Taunauk's axe fell, he could not move her. This time was the same—though now the knight held such power intrinsically.

Sword and axe crashed upon shields, neither faltering. Everfall had been made indestructible by the weeping rent, and otherworldly magic still coursed through the knight's armor.

But the blows forced Taunauk backward, staggering him with each step. For a moment, it looked as if the knight would best him, whittle him down as if Taunauk were merely a man.

But he was not just a man. He was Endroggen, and as the battle raged, Helesys felt the blood magic coursing through Taunauk as he tapped his deep well of rage. Like a bellows working the fires of a forge until it was hot enough to bend steel. He yielded less and less to the knight, until with three mighty swings, he forced her back and nearly off her feet.

The knight backpedaled, her shield arm barely capable of withstanding his axefalls.

Her desperate voice echoed over the riverbank. *"Invoco fractos sepulchra!"*

Shards of glass beneath their feet began to glow purple all across the riverbank—stretching across the horizon. It looked as if they were standing atop a starry night sky. And as the light grew beneath them, darkness bled everywhere else. The void black sky above shrank until it was oppressing and might collapse on top of them. The knight's armor grew so dark she looked like a shadow possessed.

The knight met Taunauk's blows, batting them away and raining her own down upon him. Taunauk was pushed back—

Thrown back.

And in that darkest moment, Taunauk glowed golden. In the darkness, he looked like he'd been set aflame.

Light and darkness struggled against one another. The ground burned. The sky fell until it felt like the knight had swallowed the realm.

Shadow and gold swung their blades at each other in one final blow.

Taunauk's power swelled, and he screamed. The Endroggen flared like a cataclysmic star brought to earth—his ancestors' power, magnified by a father's anguish and a son's rage.

Helesys and Shawn recoiled toward each other, away from the light. Metal screamed, and it was over.

Helesys and Shawn turned. The riverbank was as it was, merely glistening purple in the night. The knight was on her knees, heirloom axe embedded in her chest—nearly cleaved in half.

She gasped, "I choose ruin, every time," and spat at his feet.

Taunauk ripped his axe from her chest, and the knight fell. Her body and armor turned to ooze, and she seeped into the ground.

The victor stood tall, breathing heavy. "Good riddance," he said, voice as cold as stone.

~ ~ ~

Gorge of Glass

"We had your back," Shawn said.

"I know," Taunauk replied.

"But you didn't need it."

The Endroggen smirked. "I know."

The heroes walked along the glass river, ever deeper into the realm. The sky was starless—empty.

"So, you guys had history?" Shawn asked.

"Yes. She killed me once. Never again."

"I'd say you settled that matter. Decisively."

Helesys added, "With any luck, she's on the other side of the realms."

Shawn mumbled in agreement, then asked, "How did you do that at the end? That was intense."

Helesys smiled, for she already knew the answer. And she relished that her powers allowed her to glimpse something that escaped the rogue.

"The strength of my ancestors, compounded by my own rage. It is an easy thing to call upon a memory for strength, but I've never felt such power as I did then... I called upon an entire lifetime of struggle. Not just mine, but my ancestors, as well. Distilled into a single breath." Taunauk bowed his head in reverence as they walked. "My bane has become my birthright."

Silence fell between them, the only sound was the faint crunch of glass in the mud as they walked. Helesys and Shawn shared a glance, and a smile—Helesys knew that he was interning their comrade's words, as she was.

Helesys could think of no greater strength than Taunauk's, of Endroggen blood magic. To recycle deficit or pain into something new—a power greater than the sum of its parts.

All three of them had relearned painful truths as they wandered the Dungeon. And until that moment along the glasten shore, Helesys's own realizations had been almost too painful to dwell on. She pushed them aside, buried them.

Ignorantly, she had gotten herself killed on the eternal battlefield—the heir of Great House Byyra. And when she'd been given a second chance at life, she'd let herself be tricked into exile by Aradi.

Reborn a bastard child of elf and machine. A living weapon. At times, she felt little difference between herself and the monsters she had slain across the realms.

Yet, she was more. Something greater than the sum of those things.

She would turn all her slights and pain and anger to her benefit. Bend them to her will. Harness blood magic.

And together, the three would rend the god of the realms. The Wolf King would fall—Helesys swore this.

~

In the next mile, the riverbank turned completely to glass. It looked as if they walked across a mirror that had been shattered and glued back together—its surface jagged yet solid.

The wind had died, and there was not even the sensation of cold or warmth, or even smell. There must have been air to breathe, yet there was no solace in it.

"We shouldn't be here," Shawn muttered.

"There's no going back," Taunauk replied.

"I know… I just mean, we're so far away from anything *real*. The Dungeon isn't even pretending anymore."

Helesys agreed, though she gave no voice to it. There was little to guide them here. Little to see, even less magic to sense. There was the seam in the distance, and the river of souls beside them. It glowed with brilliant strobes of purple light— whatever souls had been reduced to. This alone was nauseating, and Helesys kindled strength to keep focused.

In the distance, there was a crack in the realm. A gorge cut deep into the glass.

Hours dragged on as they walked, and the gorge grew ever wider until it was miles across. As the heroes approached, darkness grew on the horizon—as if the realm was narrowing, and there was only the gorge.

"Do, uh… Do we have to go down there?" Shawn asked.

"Yes," Helesys replied without hesitation. "There is no other way forward."

They walked down the slope. The river of souls flowed down into it—frozen in a twisting waterfall. The bright light from the river played off the jagged glass walls that surrounded them.

There was no sense of danger, and so the heroes walked with weapons drawn but slacken at their sides. There was only the disorienting light, their own quiet footfalls and hesitant breath.

It wasn't until they had trekked to the bottom of the gorge that Helesys heard anything else: Faint screams or ringing glass.

Soon there were cracks in the glass where darkness seeped through. The screams grew louder, and now Helesys was sure what they were: The screams of what was left of the souls—

Helesys knew this because her voice had once been the same. When she had died and been reduced to nothing but pain and anger—when the whole of her had been burned away on the eternal battlefield.

She slowed and stopped in front of one of the cracks of darkness. Peered through.

Souls fell away, raining through the cracks and into the abyss. Beyond the black bounds of reality.

Helesys opened her senses as wide as she could. The crystalline light around her grew blinding, but so did the darkness. She focused on the latter, trying to peer beyond the veil. To find the lost souls.

And as the darkness grew, so did her dread. The souls that fell away were not lost. They were gone. They had disappeared into the void—

Into *something* beyond.

Helesys saw nothing—could see nothing—but she *felt* what was there.

The maw of something vast and incomprehensible eating thousands of broken souls.

"Helesys—" The weaver turned, suddenly aware that Taunauk had grasped her upper arm. He pulled her away from the crack in the glass. Both her comrades' faces were wrought with concern.

And it was gone. Helesys could no longer remember what she had seen through the glass. There was only the lingering feeling of dread—like a spot in her eye after staring into the sun.

~

"You shouldn't look too closely," Shawn said.

They were still walking through the gorge, but now the space had shrunk. It was barely ten feet across. To Helesys, it now felt like they were walking inside a scour in a shining glacier.

Helesys was still shaking off the lingering strain of looking through the cracks in the glass. The dread had abated, and left her with a headache. Only a headache… Helesys felt it could've been much worse.

Shawn added, "There are things mortals weren't meant to know."

Taunauk asked, "What about godlings?"

Shawn scoffed. "We have the sense not to look."

As they walked, the cracks of void continued to grow until some towered stories above them—seeming to reach from the starless sky into the abyss somewhere beneath.

The screams were growing distant. The crystal river was fading, and so many souls were lost already.

But Helesys could still hear them.

~ ~ ~

Delta

They came to the end of the gorge and the heroes walked up the slope. The river dried up, purple fading until there was nothing but the occasional flicker of purple. It seemed whatever held the realm together was breaking further.

They reached the top of the gorge and looked out over the realm.

A dessert of glass lay before them. Darkness surrounded the plane all across the horizon. Utter desolation.

Shawn asked, "Sure we're still going the right direction?"

Helesys nodded. "I can still feel the seam. We'll be there soon."

"Is it there?" Taunauk asked, sullenly. He pointed into the distance. "Do you see it?"

There was the faintest glint of light in the distance—toward the seam.

"I think so," she said.

Beside her, Taunauk's shoulders hung heavy. She had held out hope that they would find the ten thousand souls of Accaeleum. Taunauk had been so certain that they were in the realm.

But they'd been ground down by the otherworldly evil that filled the realm, that ground down all things.

Helesys reached out to feel for them, but felt nothing. And she could not bring herself to ask Taunauk, for she saw the answer on his face.

If he stopped to mourn, Helesys would've stopped to embraced him. But he trudged on.

The heroes trudged forward, and the weight of years seemed to hang on Taunauk's shoulders. His head hung low. Of all the things, it pained Helesys most to see her comrade—her friend… defeated.

Nothing else could harm him now. He was the Chosen of the Endroggen, perhaps the greatest of his people. He was the vessel of Accaelum. Only this… Only letting down those that depended on him. Ten thousand souls he had never known.

No Terran should have to bear such weight. Least of all, her friend.

~

They walked until the last stain of souls drained from the world. The desert was black sand all around them—

Save for that distant light.

The light grew as they approached. It spread, illuminating the desert.

It seemed impossibly faint.

And golden.

No one dared speak.

The light spread until it seemed to fill the desert. Golden light flickered beneath their feet—all around.

"By Movernus," Taunauk said. "I feel them. *I hear them.*"

Moments later, Rehkoros and the other few barbarian spirits stood beside Taunauk. Each were Endroggen save for two picked up during their journey across the dungeon—other cultures from across realms and time, united by their tapping of blood magic.

The desert began to rumble, and the sound of shifting glass started as a whisper and grew thunderous.

Golden light flared around them, and souls climbed from the glass. A hundred Endroggen clawed out of the ground… a thousand… more! Golden warriors surrounded them, and the rumbling ceased.

Rehkoros's voice carried across the desert. "The missing warriors of Accaelum! Even in death their souls would not be culled, and they headed toward a righteous battle."

"I don't understand, athair," Taunauk whispered.

Rehkoros walked to the nearest warrior, a young woman with long braids woven around bars of steel. Rehkoros continued, "The Endroggen sought this place, and so they were not as weak as other souls flowing through the river. The black pyramid did not pain them, did not grind them down as it did to the others."

Rehkoros turned and his voice boomed over the mass. "Brothers, sisters, your struggle has not been in vain. We have followed you across the seams of this world and others. My son, the Vessel of Accaelum, has come for you. He and the Chosen will deliver us from this place. They will face the Wolf King, and we will help them."

A tide of golden weapons swelled high and cheers rang out across the desert.

Rehkoros turned to Taunauk, and then to Helesys and Shawn. "My son, and kin of battle, it is a good day when faith is rewarded. I can think of no Endroggen more worthy to lead us, no allies more formidable. And now you have the blades of the ten thousand lost Endroggen—a force never witnessed by living or by the dead.

"Are you ready to carry us, son?"

Taunauk raised his head high, towering over nearly all the golden warriors. "I am."

One by one, the warriors walked toward him, their silhouettes vanishing inside him. With each new soul, Taunauk's skin glowed faintly golden. Soon, the warriors were walking in droves, pouring into Taunauk, and his color grew inexorably.

The warriors stepped around Helesys and Shawn, some nodding respectfully, and a few even setting a golden hand upon their shoulder in reverence. Each touch was warm— Tears welled up in Helesys's eyes; some for pride in her comrade, and some because each golden touch brought a comfort, one that seemed to melt into her very being. Beside her, even Shawn looked shaken by the procession and the feeling.

The procession was long, and when only half the souls had joined with Taunauk his skin was already a golden statue. Though he stood stoically, his chest had begun to swell with exertion. Moments later, golden steam rose from his shoulders.

Helesys had never asked if it was difficult to carry the prior handful of souls through the realms—perhaps so few had been easy for him. But now, each new soul strained him.

Even as the souls poured into Taunauk, even as his skin smoldered like fire and his chest heaved, he did not speak.

Even as golden light began to flicker and flare like oil tossed on a fire, even as his shoulders heaved and his breath grew ragged, the procession didn't stop.

Helesys's own breaths were shallow, measured with worry.

As the crowd dwindled and the desert faded to black, Taunauk blazed bright. Helesys covered her eyes—she would've thought it impossible, but Taunauk was even brighter now than when he faced the black knight—

Now he was merely holding the souls! So much power it looked like her friend might burn up. Behind the light, he grimaced, but stood tall. Teeth clenched and body shaking, but he did not wince.

And as the last souls merged with him, the light was so bright, Helesys could no longer see her friend.

At the end, the light faded until Taunauk reappeared. His skin still glowed gold—the light somewhere between a smolder and a glaring reflection of water. It pulsed through his veins and with his breath.

Rehkoros stood alone, facing his son. All other souls were gone.

Taunauk bowed his head, his shoulders quivering from exertion. "So many voices…" And as he spoke, a hundred others echoed with him.

Rehkoros nodded and put a heavy hand on Taunauk's shoulder. "I know it pains you. I can feel it. Look at me, balac." Taunauk met his father's eyes. "It will get easier to bear, as all burdens do."

Together, father and son bowed their heads, and they said, "The blade holds the warrior as much as he holds the blade."

Rehkoros vanished. Taunauk reeled backwards. The light beneath Taunauk's skin grew turbulent.

The Vessel caught himself, leaning heavy on the head of his axe. As he breathed deep, the color steadied and cooled.

When Taunauk stood and turned to them, his body was tinged a dark gold. Helesys and Shawn stared in silent awe, and ten thousand pairs of eyes stared back.

~

They walked across the barren desert—Taunauk insisted. Each step was laborious, but the barbarian wasn't deterred. Helesys's warding light shone brightly, flickering across the sand beneath their feet. They walked the utter devastation of the realm, stealing themselves for what lay ahead.

Taunauk smoldered with golden light. Occasionally it flashed brilliantly in his eyes, like a shooting star passing.

Shawn whistled idly. "So, what are the spirits saying in there?"

"Too much."

"Oh."

Helesys asked, "Can you understand them?"

Taunauk nodded slowly. "Not all at once. It feels as if I carry a city—a piece of Accaelum—in my skull. Most do not speak to me."

"Why not?" Shawn asked.

"Out of solace. Out of reverence. I am the Vessel… I was not a part of my tribe. I am not a part of Accaelum. Besides, they know I have a job to do. We're not out yet."

Helesys opened her magic sense—

The seam was close. Close enough to touch. Yet there was nothing around them. Helesys urged them forward.

Slowly, the sky grew purple, as if an alien sun were just beyond the horizon. There was no wind, but the clouds swirled above as if they were alive—throbbing and pulsing. Helesys turned away, for she saw tendrils and maws in the clouds— This was not the purple of long dead souls, but something ancient and foul.

The desert beneath their feet began to change. Light no longer danced off the powdered glass and sand beneath their feet. Now there was only ash stretched out before them.

"Is this the seam?" Shawn asked.

Helesys felt for the seam again and found they had already passed through it.

"No…" she said. "We've already passed through it. The seams are weaker here."

Shawn whispered, "Barely held together dreams.

Taunauk nodded. "No wonder the lost souls made it this far. The boundaries are so weak, it would be like stepping right into Accaelum."

Shawn asked, "So, what *is* this place?"

Helesys flared her warding light, stretching it as far as she could. Ash stretched on into the distance.

"Cover your eyes," she said.

Helesys compounded the light with the Gar of Shéslang, and the light flared so bright that even she had to squint. Light stretched off toward the horizon.

A black sea lay before them—one of ash and death. The horizon was jagged with haphazard mountain peaks. Silhouettes moved in the distance, too far to make out any detail or tell their size. Then came a bellow—a long draw, as if the realm itself were quaking. A black shadow broke the surface—something distant and titanic. It raised up through the ground like a rib bursting through skin. Then the front opened into the silhouette of a mouth—the front of a giant serpent or whale breaching the surface, and then diving beneath it again.

"Let me guess," Shawn said, "that's where we're going next."

~ ~ ~

NEXT TIME ON
*A BATTLEAXE AND
A METAL ARM*
Book 18:

Across the Ashen Sea
Available September 2022

Spoiler–Free excerpt from *BAMA 18*

Ash stretched out into the shadows.

Periodically, Helesys flared her light, pushing the darkness back to glimpse anything that might be hiding. It wasn't long before they saw the land sloshing—it seemed as if they walked across an inlet or land bridge, beset on either side by dark water.

But at a glance the water looked no different from the land on which they walked. Both were the same black and speckled gray of ash.

Helesys paused and walked to the edge of the solid land. Then she dipped the butt of the spear into the water, prodding the bottom but found none. She leaned closer, pushing the spear as deep as she dared, and still touched nothing.

"Don't fall in," she muttered, pulling the spear back. The water dripped from its surface like sludge, but fell away cleanly.

Taunauk turned to Shawn. "What manner of creatures could live here?"

Shawn feigned surprise. "Why are you asking me?"

A long bellow echoed across the realm—no doubt one of the serpents they'd glimpsed in the distance.

"Because you know more about strange realms than we," Taunauk added.

"Oh… I suppose you're right." Shawn rubbed his chin. "Things that are powerful, strange, and ancient. Things without souls or that are too stubborn to die."

Taunauk grunted. "Things we should avoid."

To be continued September 2022

Thank you for Reading

I hope you enjoyed reading this story as much as I enjoyed writing it.

If you did, I would massively appreciate a short review on Amazon or your favorite book website. Reviews are crucial for any author, and a starred review or even just a line or two can make a huge difference.

It's especially true for the start of a series. Thanks and I hope you enjoy the next one!

Looking for more Engrossing Fantasy?

You might like ***Tales from Another World,*** an ongoing short story series containing stories about sorcerers, druids, mortals, gods, thieves, and all other manner of Terrans.

The 2nd, 3rd, and 4th installments are out and they tie into the outside world of *A Battleaxe and a Metal Arm.* So, if you're looking for more engrossing fantasy stories, and if you want to know more about this fantasy universe, read on and see how deep the rabbit hole goes.

What questions do you have about *A Battleaxe and a Metal Arm?*

If you've read this far, hopefully you'll read a bit further—both in this book and across the series. I'm not sure how most authors write serials and how much of it is flying by the seat of their pants, but that's not how I do things. For all the major questions that might come up in BAMA, I already have answers for 95% of them. Same goes for the major plot points, twists and climaxes. That might sound boring to some, especially some of you other authors who enjoy variations of writing into the dark, but I think having a solid blueprint is paramount to writing a long series.

So, what questions do you have about the story? Here are a few:

1) ~~What is the dungeon?~~ It's a soul trap of overwhelming size and power. But where did it come from? Is it a force of nature or an ill-made weapon, or perhaps something else entirely? In the real world, it looks like a giant cloud with faces writhing just beneath the surface. Helesys speculates that the

reason no one remembers it is because it's so horrific their minds blot it out!

2) ~~Who was Helesys before she got trapped~~? We've learned that Helesys was both a soldier and was the oldest daughter of the elven Great House Byyra.

3) ~~Who was Taunauk before he got trapped~~? There was an omen of a blight in the Endroggen heaven, Accaelum. Taunauk is an Endroggen barbarian who was raised as a warrior and a vessel. His purpose was to one day free the trapped Endroggen souls from the Dungeon.

4) How well did they know each other beforehand?

5) How did Helesys get her metal arm? Likely through injury, amputation, and replacement. She was likely fighting in the Eternal War, the war of the Elves against the Shadowkind.

6) ~~Who is Shawn~~? He is a wisp from the plane of dreams. One who walks through the dreams of elves and humans, while being neither. He has lived as both a god and a mortal. His kind is on the run from the elder god, Nimicus.

7) Why does Shawn feel so familiar to Helesys and Taunauk? The group speculates that they were traveling together for unknown reasons. Shawn worries that they were tracking him. This could explain why Helesys and Taunauk are always reborn together, while Shawn was usually alone.

7) Who is the Wolf King and what sinister plans does he have for our heroes? How did he come to rule over the Dungeon? How does the Gatekeeper factor into all this?

8) Who is the mysterious voice encountered on the white sandy shores of Meridian? Why do they seek the death of the Wolf-King? ...And why did they choose the heroes? The Voice might be the Gatekeeper... but the truth is still unknown...

Did I miss any questions? Probably. Connect with me and other *BAMA* fans on social media and compare questions!

I've got plans. I've got answers. And I've got them on a drip-feed. Keep reading and expect to find out a little more to the mysteries with each installment. Hopefully, you're as excited about this series as I am.

Connect with the Author

If you want to stay up to date on the latest about Samuel's publishing news and blog, check out his website and consider signing up for his monthly newsletter.

www.SamuelFlemingBooks.com

Samuel can also be found on Reddit, Tiktok, and Facebook.

Samuel Fleming is a Science Fiction and Fantasy author.

He grew up in Maryland, spending most of his time swimming and writing. Swimming gave him a lot of time to daydream, so the two hobbies complemented each other well. Idle day dreams turned into stories, some of which stuck with him for years. These days he swims a little less and writes a lot more.

He loves a good story no matter the medium: Books, TV, video games, comics, tabletop RPG's, or podcasts—most of which he attempts to share with his wife and three kids, and occasionally on his blog.